This book belongs to

. . . .

. . . .

For Dan, Trini and Elijah, and Uncle Hen – PB
To my Pedigree Chums, Eri and Lucy – MM

Other books by Mei Matsuoka

Burger Boy (written by Alan Durant)

Footprints in the Snow

This paperback edition first published in 2010 by Andersen Press Ltd.
First published in Great Britain in 2009 by Andersen Press Ltd., 20 Vauxhall Bridge Road, London SW1V 2SA.
Published in Australia by Random House Australia Pty., Level 3, 100 Pacific Highway, North Sydney, NSW 2060.
Text copyright © Peter Bently, 2009. Illustrations copyright © Mei Matsuoka, 2009.
The rights of Peter Bently and Mei Matsuoka to be identified as the author and illustrator of this work
have been asserted by them in accordance with the Copyright, Designs and Patents Act, 1988.
All rights reserved. Colour separated in Switzerland by Photolitho AG, Zürich.
Printed and bound in China by G&G Offset Printing.

10   9   8   7   6   5

British Library Cataloguing in Publication Data available.
ISBN 978 1 84270 988 7
This book has been printed on acid-free paper

We cordially invite

Peter Bently & Mei Matsuoka

to write and to illustrate

the unmissable event of

The Great Dog Bottom Swap

Andersen Press

The day had arrived for the Dogs' Summer Ball!

All the dogs in the world were lined up at the hall,

Where a sign on the door said,

Now please be so kind
As to keep your coat on
but remove your behind.

Please hang up your bottom
on one of the pegs
And remember, no growling
or cocking of legs.

So as they went in - every dog, pooch and pup -
They took off their bottoms and hung them all up.

Hundreds and hundreds of little pink 'o's
All neatly arranged in methodical rows.

What a feast the dogs had at the ball on that night!
The table was quite a magnificent sight.
They dined on fresh giblets and dog-biscuit stew

With slippers and old dug-up sheep bones to chew.

Then doggy-choc ices all creamy and brown

And fresh puddle-water to wash it all down.

When the poodles had cleared all the food bowls away
It was time for some fun from the dogs' cabaret.

The pekes did a song in ridiculous hats,

And a labrador told a rude joke about cats.

Then Coco the Conjurer got a huge laugh

By pretending to saw a dalmatian in half.

"And now," Coco said, to great woofs of applause,
"It's time for the dancing, so up on your paws!"

"Look at us!"
said an
over-excited young hound
As he whisked a fox terrier
clear off the ground.

"Watch out!"   cried a sensible
boxer named Clive
As the hound and the
terrier started to jive.

They swirled and they twirled
ever faster and faster
Until -

oh dogastrophe!
what a disaster!

The twirling was more than
the afghan could handle -
He suddenly tripped and
knocked over a candle,

Which fell on the curtains,
which promptly caught fire
(Being old and quite cheap),
sending flames ever higher.

Some dogs broke the rule that
forbade hind-leg-cocking
But the fire soon spread with
a speed that was shocking.

"Don't panic!" barked Clive in a great fit of passion.
"Let's all try to leave in an orderly fashion!"
But that was an order they chose to ignore
As they scurried and scuttled like heck for the door.

As the last dog shot out of the hall with a bark
The lights all went *phut!* and the whole place went dark.
"Wait a minute!" said Clive to the panicking mutts.
"Our bottoms! Our bottoms! We must save our butts!"

So into the cloakroom they bumbled and tumbled

And soon all the bottoms were hopelessly jumbled

As every dog
grabbed the first
bottom they saw

And fled the great fire with a bum in their paw.

Luckily every dog got out alive

And no one was caught by the fire, except Clive

And some others whose tails

had been singed all away

(Which is why all those dogs

have no tails to this day).

And all the dogs' bottoms were rescued as well.
But because of the darkness no doggy could tell

Whose bottom was whose in the panic and scrum
So each dog went home with another dog's bum.

And ever since then, when a pair of dogs meet

In the park or the playground, the woods or the street,

Each dog gives the other dog's bottom a sniff

To see if it has the particular whiff

Of the bottom they lost on the night of the ball
When the dogs hung their bums on the hooks in the hall.

If you enjoyed this, you'll also love:

The Great Balloon Hullaballoo

BY PETER BENTLY & MEI MATSUOKA

ISBN 9781849395601

'Matsuoka's distinctive style of illustration perfectly
complements Bently's wicked humour.' DAILY MAIL

The Great Sheep Shenanigans

BY PETER BENTLY & MEI MATSUOKA

ISBN 9781849393843

'Hilarious read-aloud romp!'
THE BOOKSELLER

Burger Boy

BY MEI MATSUOKA

ISBN 9781842705377

'Its witty rhymes and sprightly illustrations will definitely
entertain everyone.' EVENING STANDARD